DUDLEY PUBLIC LIBRARIES

The loan of this book may be renewed if not required by other readers, by contacting the library from which it was borrowed.

D1428733

000003065353

About Diffusion books

Diffusion publishes books for adults who are emerging readers. There are two series:

 Books in the Diamond series are ideally suited to those who are relatively new to reading or who have not practised their reading skills for some time (approximately Entry Level 2 to 3 in adult literacy levels).

 Books in the Star series are for those who are ready for the next step. These books will help to build confidence and inspire readers to tackle longer books (approximately Entry Level 3 to Level 1 in adult literacy levels).

Other books available in the Diamond series are:

Uprising by Alex Wheatle

Space Ark by Rob Childs

Snake by Matt Dickinson

Breaking the Chain by Darren Richards

Lost at Sea by Joel Smith

Books available in the Star series are:

Not Such a Bargain by Toby Forward

Barcelona Away by Tom Palmer

Forty-six Quid and a Bag of Dirty Washing by Andy Croft

Bare Freedom by Andy Croft

One Shot by Lena Semaan

Nowhere to Run by Michael Crowley

Fans

Niall Griffiths

diffusion

First published in Great Britain in 2017

Diffusion
an imprint of SPCK
36 Causton Street
London SW1P 4ST
www.spck.org.uk

ISBN 978–1–908713–13–1
eBook ISBN 978–1–908713–24–7

Contents

1
Off to the match

Jerry was on his way to pick up Stevie, his son. They were going to watch a football game.

Stevie was waiting with his mother, Jean, on the steps of the museum. This was the place they always met on the days when Jerry could see his son.

Sometimes they looked around the museum, because Stevie loved the dinosaur skeletons. Sometimes they went to the beach.

But today they would be watching the football. An important game was on. Liverpool were playing their oldest rivals, Everton.

The sun was shining brightly and seagulls were flying overhead. Stevie was eating an ice cream. It was chocolate ice cream, which was his favourite.

Jerry said hello to his ex-wife and hugged his son, who had brown ice cream all round his mouth. Jerry took a tissue out of his pocket and wiped it off.

'Make sure you bring him back here by six o'clock,' said Jean.

This was fine with Jerry. It was an early kick-off so they had plenty of time.

'I will,' Jerry said.

'And look after him,' Jean said. 'Make sure he's safe. There can be trouble at these games. There was trouble at the last match.'

'Of course I'll keep him safe,' Jerry said. 'He's my son too.'

'I know he is,' said Jean, and bent down to kiss the top of Stevie's head.

'Have a good time and look after your dad,' she said, and Stevie nodded. 'I hope Liverpool win,' Jean said.

'We will,' Stevie said.

Jerry said goodbye to Jean and took Stevie's hand. He led Stevie over the road to the bus stop. Jean watched them go. At the bus stop they turned and waved to her. She waved back and walked away.

Stevie's hand was sticky from the ice cream so Jerry had to use a tissue again.

'I wish you and mum were still friends,' Stevie said as his dad was wiping his hand.

'We are still friends,' said Jerry.

'Well, I wish you still lived with each other,' said Stevie.

'So do I, sometimes,' Jerry said. 'But sometimes people fall out of love with each other. They don't start to hate each other, it's just that they think they would be happier not living together. Do you understand?'

Stevie nodded, but Jerry knew that he didn't really understand. He was too young.

Talking about this always made Stevie sad. Jerry bent down to look into his face and said, 'But your mum and I will always be glad that we met each other, and do you know why? Because of you. If we had never met each other then we would not have had you.'

'But if you still lived with Mum, I could see you every day,' Stevie said.

'I know,' Jerry said. 'And I would like to see you every day. But then your mum and I would see each other every day as well, which means that we would argue more.'

'But why?' Stevie asked.

'We just would,' Jerry said. 'You will understand when you get older. But just remember this. Your mum and I both think you're the best little boy in the world.'

This seemed to cheer Stevie up.

The bus came, but before they got on it Jerry looked through the windows to see if it was full of Everton supporters. There was no way that he would get on a bus full of rival fans.

There were no Everton supporters on the bus, so he and Stevie got on. They paid their fare and set off for the ground.

What do you think?

- Why did Jerry check to see whether or not the bus was full of Everton supporters before he and Stevie got on it?

- What reason does Jerry give to Stevie for why he and his mother don't live together any more? Do you think it's a good explanation?

- If you need to talk to a young child about something difficult, what might you need to think about?

2

Liverpool v. Everton

The city of Liverpool is home to two football clubs, Liverpool and Everton. Matches between them are always sold out. Today's match was being played at Anfield, Liverpool's stadium.

Jerry and Stevie got off the bus at the stadium. There were thousands of people going to the match.

On the streets around the stadium people were selling scarves and souvenirs for both teams.

There was a smell of burgers and onions. There were also lots of police. Some were on foot and some were on horses.

One horse backed away from a group of noisy young men, towards Stevie, who grabbed hold of Jerry's leg.

'It's OK,' Jerry said to Stevie. 'Stay close to me. The horse doesn't want to hurt you. It was just a bit frightened, that's all.'

The last time they had come to one of these games, Stevie had been small enough to be carried on Jerry's shoulders. He had felt safe like that, when he was higher than the other people, and at the same level as the policemen on the horses.

But now he was too big to be carried on his dad's shoulders. It was frightening for him with all the legs moving around him.

All he could see were the legs of people and the legs of the horses. It felt a bit like being lost in a forest.

Most of the fans were walking down the middle of the road. Jerry took his son on to the pavement, closer to the houses. There weren't so many people there.

Jerry and Stevie could see into some of the houses. In one house, there was a bunch of flowers in the window and in another house there was a ginger cat. Jerry pointed out the cat to Stevie and Stevie smiled because he liked cats. He had a cat at home, called Shankly. Shankly was also ginger.

At another house, the window was open and an old man was leaning out with his arms on the windowsill. He was wearing an LFC hat and when he saw Stevie he winked.

'Good luck,' the old man said. 'Hope we win.'

'We will,' Stevie said.

The old man laughed and so did Jerry.

It would be fine today, Jerry thought. The sun was out and the crowd seemed happy. Stevie seemed happy too. It was a good day to watch a football game.

Today was going to be a good day, Jerry thought again. And then he heard a noise.

What do you think?

- Have you ever been in a big crowd? How did you feel?

- Do you support a football team (or another sports team)? What made you support that team?

- What do you think it would be like to live in a city that is home to two rival football teams? What issues might arise?

3

The crowd turns

The noise Jerry heard wasn't a good one. It wasn't a happy cheer, like when a goal is scored. It wasn't like a lot of people laughing. It was more like a big roar, like a lot of people roaring and shouting at the same time. And it was getting louder.

'What's that noise?' Stevie asked.

'I don't know,' said Jerry. 'But let's just wait here for a moment.'

Jerry was worried by the noise. He had heard that kind of noise before, and he knew it meant that trouble was on the way.

Jerry took his son's hand and stood back from the crowd, close to the houses. This seemed the safest place, and all of a sudden he had begun to feel a bit unsafe.

The roar was getting louder. The crowd had stopped walking. They had been walking into the roar, but now the roar was moving into them. The policemen turned their horses around to face the noise.

'What's going on?' asked Stevie.

But Jerry did not hear him because he was watching the policemen on their horses. Some of them were speaking into their radios.

Some more policemen appeared. They were wearing helmets and riot gear.

Some were holding batons. They were getting out of cars and vans and Jerry could hear sirens.

Jerry felt Stevie cling on to his leg. He put his hand on his son's head to try to make him feel a bit safer.

And then the roar suddenly became very loud and started moving towards them very quickly. Everyone in the crowd turned and ran away as fast as they could.

The policemen on their horses began to charge towards the sound. So did the policemen in riot gear.

Jerry felt as though the ground was shaking with all the running people and horses.

Jerry saw a man fall over and hit his head on the kerb. He wanted to go to help him but somebody else picked him up and carried on running.

He ran while holding the man up. Jerry wasn't sure if he could have helped the man anyway because he was too busy looking out for Stevie.

Jerry had dreaded this moment. Liverpool and Everton fans were usually quite friendly these days, with just a bit of name-calling, but Jerry knew that they could also be very violent.

Jerry always told Stevie to be careful of Everton fans because they could cause trouble, but he hoped that his son would never actually see it.

'Run! Get away!' shouted a woman holding a baby.

Jerry thought this was a good idea. He grabbed Stevie's hand, ready to start running away with the rest of the crowd.

Just then he saw something flying through the air towards him. He watched it and as it got closer he saw that it was a bottle.

The bottle smashed on the road. Without thinking, Jerry put his hands over his face to protect himself from the glass.

When he went to take Stevie's hand again, Stevie wasn't there.

What do you think?

- Do you think young children should go to watch football matches? Why or why not?

- Why do you think violence sometimes breaks out between fans of different teams?

- Can you think of a time when you were frightened (as an adult or a child)? Knowing what you know now, what advice would you give the frightened you?

4
Lost and found

Jerry could not see Stevie. He began to panic.

He shouted his son's name. 'Stevie! Steeee-vie!'

He shouted as loud as he could but a lot of
people were shouting at the same time. A lot of
people were running, too, and so were the horses.
Everything was loud. Everybody was panicking.

Jerry moved away from the houses, into the road
and into the crowd, searching. He was looking for
a small boy in a black jacket and a Liverpool shirt.

People who were trying to get away from the fighting banged into him. He was knocked this way and that, to the left and then to the right.

All the time he was shouting his son's name. 'Steeee-vie!'

Jerry was starting to panic now. His head was spinning and he was so confused. He didn't know which way was forward and which way was back. He didn't know what to do.

Jerry was swept up with the crowd and carried down the road. He fell on to his hands and knees but just managed to get back to his feet before he was trampled. He could hear the sounds of fighting behind him, people shouting and screaming, glass breaking.

Everything was happening so quickly. Everything was moving so fast, and everything was so loud.

Through the crowd he saw a small boy crouched down behind a car on the other side of the road. Was it Stevie?

Jerry could not be sure because the boy had his head in his hands. But the boy's hair was the same colour as Stevie's and he was wearing a black jacket.

Jerry fought his way through the running crowd. It was hard, because he was moving across the crowd. He almost fell to the ground twice, but he managed to reach the boy.

Jerry crouched down beside the boy. He put his arm over the boy's shoulders to protect him. He was panting for breath and there was sweat in his eyes, but both he and his son were safe here behind the car.

'Thank God I found you,' Jerry said. 'Are you OK, Stevie?'

Jerry looked down at the boy and the boy looked up at him. The boy was not his son.

'I'm not Stevie. I'm Duncan,' said the boy. 'And I want my dad.'

What do you think?

- How do you think Jerry feels when he can't find Stevie?

- Have you ever been lost or lost someone else? How did you feel?

- Jerry's 'head was spinning and he was so confused'. Do you ever feel like this? What are some good ways of coping if you do?

5

Never trust a man in a red shirt

Jerry could see that the little boy was scared.

Duncan's eyes were big and his lip was trembling as if he was about to cry.

'It's OK,' Jerry said. 'We are going to be all right.'

Duncan looked up at Jerry's face. Jerry looked down at him and saw that underneath Duncan's jacket was a blue Everton shirt.

'But you are one of them,' Duncan said. 'My dad told me that you don't like Everton fans like me.'

'Did he? Well, that's just daft,' Jerry said.

'My dad's not daft,' said Duncan. 'Don't you call my dad daft.' He began to cry.

'I'm sorry,' Jerry said. 'I didn't mean that your dad is daft. I just mean that you don't need to be afraid of me. I'm not going to hurt you.'

And then Jerry remembered that he had often told Stevie not to trust Everton fans. And now, here he was with a lost little boy who was scared of him.

Duncan was scared and alone and he didn't trust Jerry. Duncan's dad had probably told him not to trust fans who wore red, and that was why he was scared of Jerry. This made Jerry feel very bad inside.

There was another roar. It sounded like people were fighting on the other side of the car.

Duncan's shoulders shook as he cried.

Jerry remembered that he had two Kit Kats in his pocket. He had been saving them for Stevie and himself for half-time. He took one out and held it out to Duncan.

'Do you like Kit Kats?' he asked. 'You can have one.'

Duncan took it and said, 'Thank you.'

'Kit Kats are my little boy's favourites,' Jerry said. 'You see, I have a little boy the same age as you. He's lost as well. I'm very worried about him. We got separated when all the trouble kicked off.'

Duncan asked, 'Will you help me find my dad?'

'I will,' said Jerry. 'Let's wait for the trouble to die down and then we will find a policeman. I'm sure your dad will be fine. I hope my little boy is too.'

Jerry was having to shout so that he could be heard over the noise. He saw another bottle come through the air and explode on the pavement near them.

The car they were hiding behind shook as something fell against it. Jerry was worried that they were not safe there any more.

Jerry looked around for somewhere to run to. Down the street he saw the man in the LFC hat leaning out of his window, waving at him.

'Are you all right?' the man shouted.

'The little boy is terrified!' Jerry shouted back.

Jerry was frightened too, but he did not tell the man that.

'I can see that the mob is going away,' the man said. 'More police are coming. Stay there and you will be safe.'

The man went back inside his house and closed the window.

Jerry could hear that things were getting quieter. But Duncan was still shaking with fear.

Jerry wanted to help him to feel better but he didn't know what to do or say. He just said the first thing that came into his head.

'What's your favourite chocolate bar?' he asked.

'Double Decker,' said Duncan. 'But Kit Kats are my second favourite.'

Jerry smiled at Duncan. Duncan did not smile back.

Jerry hoped that Stevie was OK. He hoped that someone had found him and was keeping him safe, like he was keeping Duncan safe. Two scared little boys.

What do you think?

- Why does Jerry feel bad inside when he sees that Duncan is scared of him?

- In the story, Liverpool and Everton fans both have prejudices against the other. What other prejudices do we find in our society? (A person has a 'prejudice' when they dislike somebody they don't know for being different from them.)

- What can you do to help break down prejudices that other people may have against you? What can you do to help overcome your own prejudices against others?

6
Cats and dogs

Jerry looked at his watch. He saw that there was only half an hour until kick-off.

By now, the noise of the crowd had died down. Jerry got up and looked over the top of the car that he and Duncan were hiding behind. The crowd was moving away from them, down the road.

Then Jerry heard the sound of an ambulance.

This worried him because he thought of Stevie. He might be hurt. He hoped his son was safe.

He also thought of Duncan's dad. He must be hoping that his son was safe too.

The siren got louder.

Duncan looked frightened again. Jerry didn't want this little boy to be frightened. He saw a cat hiding under another car. This cat was black. In the darkness under the car, Jerry could see his green eyes.

'Look at the cat,' he said to Duncan. 'Do you like cats?'

Duncan nodded.

'So does my little boy,' said Jerry. 'He's got a cat at home, a ginger one. He loves him. Can you guess what he's called?'

Duncan shook his head.

'He's called Shankly,' Jerry said. 'Have you got a cat?'

'No,' said Duncan. 'We have got a dog.'

'What's he called?' asked Jerry.

'Moyesie,' said Duncan.

Jerry laughed. Of course an Everton fan would have a pet called Moyesie, or maybe Dixie or something.

'What kind of dog is he?' asked Jerry.

'He's a brown dog,' said Duncan.

'I mean what breed,' said Jerry. 'Do you know what breed he is?'

'He's a mix,' Duncan said. 'My dad calls him a mong, a mongler, or something.'

'A mongrel,' Jerry said, to help Duncan out. 'That's the name for a dog that is a mixture of breeds. Does he fetch sticks?'

Duncan nodded. 'And he chases squirrels up trees,' he said. 'And he eats slippers.'

This made Jerry laugh again and he was pleased to see that Duncan gave a little smile.

'Moyesie eats your slippers?' asked Jerry.

'Not mine,' Duncan said, 'because I hide mine. When I'm not wearing my slippers, I put them on top of the wardrobe.'

'So whose slippers does he eat?' asked Jerry, happy to keep Duncan talking.

'My dad's slippers,' said Duncan. 'He always eats them.'

'He must like the taste,' said Jerry.

Now Duncan laughed and Jerry felt good. It pleased him to make this lost boy laugh. He hoped that Stevie, wherever he was, was laughing too.

What do you think?

- Why do you think Jerry talks to Duncan about cats and dogs?

- If someone is frightened, what could you do to help them?

- If you could have any pet, what would it be and what would you call it?

7

The wrong son

Jerry saw that he and Duncan were still holding their Kit Kats. They had forgotten to eat them. They had been talking instead.

So he unwrapped his and ate it and Duncan did the same. Then Jerry put the wrappers in his pocket. He could see a rubbish bin, but it was quite a way down the road, and he didn't want to go over to it and leave Duncan on his own.

The cat had gone from under the other car. The noise of the ambulance had gone too and so had the sound of the fighting.

Jerry could no longer hear shouting or breaking glass. It was much quieter now. Everything was calm again.

Jerry looked at his watch. It was not long until kick-off.

'I think we are safe now,' he said. 'Shall we go and see if we can find a policeman?'

Duncan nodded.

'Come on, then,' said Jerry. 'He might be able to help me find my son. And help you find your dad.'

'I hope so,' said Duncan.

They stood up. Jerry felt an ache in his knees because he had been crouching for so long.

Duncan was fine, of course, because he was much younger than Jerry.

The road on the other side of the car was full of broken bottles and bricks. Jerry saw that a few cars had had their windows smashed in and doors dented. But he could not see any blood. He was glad of that.

The policemen on horses had gone but there was a big police car, one of those ones with cages across its windows. Standing next to it was a policeman. He was wearing normal police uniform, not riot gear. Jerry went over to him.

'Hello,' Jerry said to the policeman. 'I need some help.'

The policeman nodded. He had a moustache and a shaven head and tattoos on his arms. Jerry thought that he looked tough.

'I have lost my son,' Jerry said.

The policeman looked down at Duncan and then back up at Jerry.

'Well, who is that, then?' he said.

'He's not my son. I have been looking after him,' Jerry said. 'You see, when it all kicked off, I lost my own son in the crowd, but I found this little lad. He has lost his dad. So, I'm looking for my son and he's looking for his dad.'

The policeman looked down at Duncan. 'Is that right?' he asked.

Duncan nodded.

'OK,' the policeman said. 'Let me see what I can do. You two wait here and I'll put a call out on the radio.'

The policeman went round to the other side of the police car. Jerry watched him and saw that hanging from his belt there was a baton, handcuffs and pepper spray. He thought that if Duncan saw these he might be frightened again.

He looked down at the boy, but Duncan didn't seem worried by them at all. Maybe, if he had been to lots of football games, he was used to seeing the police. Maybe he felt safe now that the policeman was helping them.

'Are you OK?' Jerry asked Duncan.

Duncan nodded again.

'You will soon be back with your dad,' Jerry said.

The policeman came back. He was smiling. 'You two are in luck,' he said.

What do you think?

- Why did Jerry ask the policeman for help?

- Would you ever ask the police for help? When might you do so?

- Duncan is not worried about the policeman's baton, handcuffs and pepper spray and Jerry thinks it is because he is used to seeing them. Why might seeing something often make it less worrying? Why might this be a good thing, and why might it not?

8

Reunited

The policeman told Jerry and Duncan that he had spoken to another officer on the radio. This officer was not far away, only around the corner. She was with a man and a small boy.

The man was looking for his son and the boy was looking for his dad. The boy's name was Stevie. The man's missing son was called Duncan.

'That's me!' said Duncan. 'My name is Duncan!'

'And what's your father's name?' asked the policeman.

'Dad,' said Duncan. The policeman smiled at Jerry.

'But what's his proper name?' the policeman asked. 'What do people call him who aren't his kids?'

'Gary,' said Duncan.

The policeman nodded. 'In that case, we have found your dad,' he said.

Duncan looked up at Jerry and gave him a great big smile. Jerry smiled at Duncan too.

Then Jerry saw a man and a boy walking down the road towards them. He did not know the man but he knew who the boy was.

Jerry called out Stevie's name. At the same time, the other man, who must be Gary, called out Duncan's name. The two small boys ran to their fathers and hugged them tightly.

'I'm so glad you're safe,' Jerry said to Stevie. 'I was worried sick about you. Are you OK?'

He held Stevie by his shoulders and looked into his face. He asked him again if he was OK and Stevie nodded.

'The nice man looked after me,' Stevie said, pointing at Duncan's dad.

Jerry looked at Gary. Gary was doing the same as Jerry. He was looking into his son's face and asking him if he was all right.

Duncan did the same thing as Stevie. He nodded and told his dad that the nice man had looked after him.

Jerry and Gary looked at each other. Jerry saw Gary's Everton shirt and Gary saw Jerry's Liverpool shirt. They looked at both boys and smiled.

Stevie and Duncan grinned at each other. They stood together on a street covered with bricks and bottles and glass. They were so happy to be back with their dads.

Jerry spoke first. 'Thanks for looking after my son,' he said.

'Same to you,' said Gary, and held out his hand.

The two men shook hands.

'Now, you had all better get into the ground,' the policeman said.

Everyone had forgotten he was there.

'Kick-off is in ten minutes,' the policemen told them. 'You don't want to miss it, do you?'

What do you think?

- How do you think Jerry feels when he is reunited with Stevie?

- What do you think Jerry feels when he sees Gary's Everton T-shirt?

- In what ways has Jerry been 'a nice man'?

9
Home fans

They walked down the road towards the ground. Jerry walked with Stevie and Gary walked with Duncan. They stepped over the bricks and broken glass on the road.

As they got near to the ground the noise from inside got louder. This time it was a happy noise. The crowds were cheering. The players must be coming out of the tunnels.

They all walked a bit faster.

Jerry asked his son if he had been scared when the trouble started and Jerry had lost him.

'I was at first,' Stevie said, 'because I didn't know where you had gone. But the nice man looked after me. I was hiding behind a car because I felt safe there. He sat down by me and talked to me. And he gave me a Double Decker.'

'Did he?' Jerry said with a smile. 'Was it nice?'

'Yes, but not as nice as a Kit Kat,' Stevie said. 'And he told me about his dog. It eats slippers.'

Jerry laughed. He remembered Duncan laughing too, when they were hiding behind the car.

Jerry did not know what he would tell Jean when he took Stevie back to her. She would know there had been trouble and would be upset. But she would be pleased that her son had been looked after.

Jerry thought about what had happened. Today, it was an Everton fan who had kept Stevie safe. And even though Jerry had loved Liverpool all his life, he had kept Duncan, an Everton fan, safe too. It didn't really matter who had caused the trouble before today's match. What really mattered was who had done the protecting, keeping the boys safe.

He had been wrong to tell Stevie not to trust Everton fans.

Of course, there are some fans of both teams who cause trouble and want to fight. But in their hearts, most fans are good. They love their team and they love their children. They want to keep all children safe from harm, including children who support the other team. They just want to take their kids to watch the football and to have fun.

Jerry wondered if Gary was thinking the same thing.

At the ground, they were going different ways. Jerry and Stevie were going to the home supporters gates and Gary and Duncan were going to the away supporters gates.

But, Jerry thought, they were all home supporters really. After all, the same city was home to both football teams and to both groups of fans.

As they set off for their different gates, Jerry called out to Gary and Duncan, 'Good luck!'

Gary turned and waved his arm. 'Good luck!' he shouted back.

And then they all went inside the ground, just in time for kick-off.

What do you think?

- How far do you agree with Jerry that Liverpool fans and Everton fans are no better or worse than each other, just different?

- Can you think of any other 'old rivals', such as rival gangs or people from different countries? Could the same be said of them?

- In the end, Jerry and Gary wish each other good luck. Why is it important for players and fans to be 'good sports' (that is, to play fair, accept winning and losing, and to stay friendly)?

- Do you think you are a 'good sport'? Why?

Books available in the Diamond series

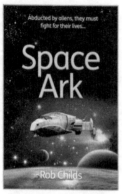

Space Ark

by Rob Childs (ISBN: 978 1 908713 11 7)

Ben and his family are walking in the woods when they are thrown to the ground by a dazzling light. Ben wakes up to find they have been abducted by aliens. Will Ben be able to defeat the aliens and save his family before it is too late?

Snake

by Matt Dickinson (ISBN: 978 1 908713 12 4)

Liam loves visiting the local pet shop and is desperate to have his own snake. Then one day, Mr Nash, the owner of the shop, just disappears. What has happened to Mr Nash? And how far will Liam go to get what he wants?

Fans

by Niall Griffiths (ISBN: 978 1 908713 13 1)

Jerry is excited about taking his young son Stevie to watch the big match. But when trouble breaks out between the fans, Jerry and Stevie can't escape the shouting, fighting and flying glass. And then Stevie gets lost in the crowd. What will Jerry do next? And what will happen to Stevie?

Breaking the Chain

by Darren Richards (ISBN: 978 1 908713 08 7)

Ken had a happy life. But then he found out a secret that changed everything. Now he is in prison for murder. Then Ken meets the new lad on the wing, Josh. Why does Ken tell Josh his secret? And could it be the key to their freedom?

Lost at Sea

by Joel Smith (ISBN: 978 1 908713 09 4)

Alec loves his job in the Royal Navy. His new mission is to save refugees from unsafe boats. But when a daring rescue attempt goes wrong, Alec is the one who needs saving. Who will come to help him?

Uprising: A true story

by Alex Wheatle (ISBN 978 1 908713 10 0)

Alex had a tough start in life. He grew up in care until he was fourteen, when he was sent to live in a hostel in Brixton. After being sent to prison for taking part in the Brixton Uprising, Alex's future seemed hopeless. But then something happened to change his life…

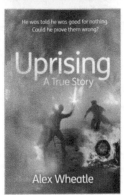

You can order these books by writing to Diffusion, SPCK, 36 Causton Street, London SW1P 4ST or visiting www.spck.org.uk/what-we-do/prison-fiction/